Twinkle
Tames a Dragon

PERFECT Pets

Katharine Holabird and Sarah Warburton

Hodder
Children's
Books

Twinkle wanted a pet more than anything,
and so did her best friends Pippa and Lulu.

Twinkle even made up a special song:

"I've waited and wished
for such a long time...
for a sweet little pet who
will truly be mine!"

When Fairy Godmother heard Twinkle's song, she invited all three fairies to the palace. "You're now old enough to take care of a pet," she said, "so let's make your wishes come true."

"Abracadabra, skiddledee~pie, this pet loves to swoop and fly!"

Fairy Godmother waved her wand, and in a sparkly flash
a gorgeous butterfly appeared next to Pippa.

"Fairytastic!
I LOVE butterflies!"
said Pippa.

Fairy Godmother waved her wand again.

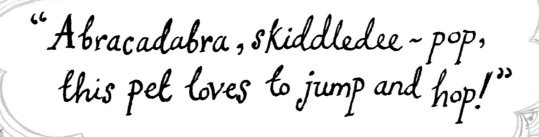

"Abracadabra, skiddledee ~ pop,
this pet loves to jump and hop!"

A glittery ladybird
landed on Lulu's head.
"Ooooh, lovely!"
said Lulu.

Twinkle couldn't wait for her sweet little pet to arrive.

"Abracadabra, skiddledee~day,
this pet loves to run and play!"

Fairy Godmother
swooshed her
wand and...

The walls shook, the chandelier swayed, purple smoke poured
out of the fireplace, and then out popped...

...a little dragon!

"Fiddlesticks and fairycakes!" exclaimed Twinkle. "I really wanted something cute and fluffy, **not** a dragon!"

"He just needs a little taming, that's all," said
Fairy Godmother, avoiding the puffs of smoke.
"Now, why don't you all bring your pets to Fairy
Pet Day? There'll be prizes and fun for everyone!"

But Scruffy needed more than just a bit of taming…

He gobbled up Twinkle's fairy cakes, left muddy footprints everywhere and even chewed her best slippers!

POD SWEET POD

Twinkle decided there was only one thing for it...

...Dragon Obedience Class!

"Fetch the ball," said Twinkle, as Scruffy galloped past her.

"Fly over the fence," shouted Twinkle, as the little dragon snored noisily in the corner.

"Sit," cried Twinkle, as Scruffy ran around in circles.

"Oh dear," said Twinkle, tickling Scruffy's tummy, "I'll never be able to tame you in time!"

When Fairy Pet Day at the Palace arrived,
Twinkle scrubbed and brushed Scruffy until his scales
were shining. She tied a pretty ribbon in his topknot,
and gave him a fancy new collar.

"You'll surely win a prize for being cute even if you are the naughtiest dragon in class," Twinkle said.

But on the way to the palace, Scruffy jumped in a great big puddle and splashed mud everywhere!

"Oh no!" sighed Twinkle.
"We'll never win anything now."

Fairy Pet Day

The palace was crowded with fairies and their pets. Everyone applauded as Pippa's butterfly won a prize for prettiest pet, and Lulu's ladybird won a prize for her clever tricks.

It was soon time for the best-trained pet award. Twinkle knew Scruffy didn't have a chance, but she loved her new pet anyway.

"Just do your best, Scruffy," she whispered.

Scruffy cocked his ears and gazed sweetly at
Twinkle as she tossed a ball high into the sky.

"Go, Scruffy!"
Twinkle shouted.
Scruffy zoomed off like a rocket,

did a few loop-the-loops,

and disappeared...

But then the little dragon raced back through the clouds
and dropped the ball at Twinkle's feet.

"Hooray!" everyone cheered.

"Congratulations," said Fairy Godmother as she gave Twinkle and Scruffy their prize, "what a well tamed little dragon."

Twinkle was so proud. Her wings glowed rainbow colours
and she sang happily to Scruffy:

BEST TAMED PET

"Scruffy is my dragon
and he loves to run and play...
He's the best pal ever, and
I love him more each day!"

Tweeter

Bumpy

Bristle

Nutter

Snuffles

Flitter

Hopper